Now, *That's* a Trick

flash fiction by

Dawn Sperber

Finishing Line Press
Georgetown, Kentucky

Now, *That's* a Trick

For my mom

ACKNOWLEDGMENTS

"Now, That's a Trick" first appeared in *Zizzle Literary*, 2021.

"If the River Men Take You" first appeared in *Annalemma*, 2009.

"We've Already Been Invented" first appeared in *The Santa Fe Reporter*, fiction contest winner, 2012.

"Our Master of Psalmody" first appeared in *[PANK] Magazine* #8.2, 2013.

"Youth" first appeared in *flashquake* #9.2, 2009.

"Sulfur Steam" first appeared in *Moon Milk Review* (now *The Doctor T. J. Eckleburg Review*), November 2010.

"You Could Measure It Perfectly" first appeared in *Hunger Mountain* #13, 2008.

"Why the Moon" first appeared in *The Pedestal Magazine* #33, 2006.

"Wind in a Ring Box" first appeared in *Gargoyle* #57, 2011.

"Wish on the Ring's Eye" first appeared on *Whidbey Writers' Student Choice Awards* website, June 2011.

Publisher: Leah Huete de Maines
Editor: Christen Kincaid
Cover Art: Alexandra Eldridge
Author Photo: Matti Greenman and Dawn Sperber
Cover Design: Elizabeth Maines McCleavy

Table of Contents

Now, *That's* a Trick

Lightning got drawn down by the coins in his shirt pocket, maybe. What you carry can have far-reaching effects.

The night of the monsoon party, I didn't have any pockets. But as John approached along the rainy Corrales path, his pockets' jingling announced him. I knew the sound well after so many replays of our few memories.

There was the bus stop morning when we peered out at the white early sky, sharing the bench, and I could've sworn I heard his thoughts clinking. Dawn birds sang, and John's thoughts tinkled as we created a kind bus-stop intimacy, taking in the day. Once I'd gotten off at my stop for work, I realized it must have been his pocket shifting with his breathing. But I loved that morning when I'd believed his thinking made the clinkings.

Then, one time at the New Mexico State Fair, I spotted him from the air while I was circling in the Ferris wheel and I learned something. John's boots might have a confident stride, but whenever he had a choice—to turn left or right, or risk his life on a rollercoaster—he left his fate to heads or tails.

He had the noble mystery of a traveler, but he was somehow local. I did a triple-take when his antique Ford truck pulled up at my dad's stable and he became a summer ranch-hand. I'd catch him sometimes, doing magic tricks under the grandfather cottonwoods in the dirt parking lot. He'd pull a coin from behind someone's ear, make it disappear with a turn of his wrist, and somehow reveal it in his other hand.

He could make a coin spin and levitate in the air, and I never knew how he did it. He could do it with bottle-caps too. Seemed like half the time he had a coin rippling over his fingers, trickling up and down. When he turned his head, I checked him for invisible wiring. I learned to puppeteer at Jemez summer camp and it gave me ideas. But John's tricks didn't rely on fishing line.

I was intrigued, but a bit shy, so it was easier to just rush to work and walk past him. But the day the summer's long drought finally broke, so did my patience with bad routines. I quit my hostess job at Kountry Kitchen, cut up my polyester dress, along with a pile of other old uniforms, and sewed them together into a paneled, A-line skirt. It turned out cute, and I wore it the next night to the monsoon party.

I never expected to see John there. By the time he arrived, clinking up the path to the old soccer field, the party was packed with folks from the nearby ranches and small towns. The rain poured as we crowded in the candlelit yurt, but I still heard him approach, and then he bent his head under the low door and joined us in the circle.

Thunder broke, and people laughed and screamed as an electric storm came on strong. Lightning branched across the sky, and John rose from our circle and wandered off, like he just couldn't stay away from those attraction lines. He strode into the field with his hands raised to the flashing sky. No one else noticed him, but I leaned back, watching. It was like he'd found the original currents that fueled his tricks. He stood beneath the white crackling, his mouth open to catch a drink of rain.

It was totally silent when the lightning bolt struck. A flash: John's arms outstretched, his hair straight up, eyes bright as pennies. The bolt winked out with a shaking sonic boom, and he crumpled like a dollar bill tossed down.

I bunched up my skirt of old uniforms, already heavy with rain, and slid to my knees in the grass and red dirt with my skirt fanned around where he lay steaming. His eyelashes dripped, and rain plocked on his soaked Western shirt. Thinking the worst, I started a prayer, but that John sure has a charmed life. He coughed out a puff of smoke and sat up, mystified.

Years of my disappointment in the world dissolved. The gravity of life's tragedies lifted as I looked at him—alive—there in front of me. And I said, "Now, *that's* a trick."

"My chest," he whispered. A trickle of smoke curled through his pearled buttons.

As the raindrops hit, I popped his line of button-snaps and yanked his shirt off. Lightning crashed, and his chest shone in the light. I touched him, and he moaned.

On his chest, my fingers slid across metal. The coins claimed him; they must have loved him too. In the darkness, just to the left of his breastbone, I saw a melted pool of silver, faintly heart-shaped.

He touched it with his fingertips, as he looked at me stupefied. I helped him to his feet while the downfall continued. He kept staring, lips parted.

"You're okay?" I asked.

The melted silver heart on his chest winked with his breathing, reflecting lights, like a tossed-up coin, flipping in midair.

Why did I feel like I was asking if he'd love me?

"Can't tell yet," he said.

I chewed the inside of my cheek, nodded. I picked up a coin from the wet grass and stuck it under my waistband.

He watched me, then smiled like a show's finale. "Yeah, yeah, definitely," he corrected. And my heart was a sparkler in the night.

That's how I remember it, anyway. The way love hits, it's frighteningly dramatic. Everything turns to poetry and impact, at least briefly.

I still carry that coin I picked up that night, years after John and I grew up and into different people, long after I left town. Life changes, but even now I still always sew a little pocket in my skirts and dresses.

We have choices about what we carry with us. I carry my enchantment.

*

If the River Men Take You

I'm sure Rusty won't believe me. I bet he'll look for the psychological reasons, the passive aggression in losing my engagement ring, "supposedly," I imagine him saying with wide nostrils, "by mistake." Then he'll staccato, "While Crossing Our Same Bridge," meaning where we met.

I don't know how to answer people who are so suspicious. I didn't throw the ring in. It's not like I wanted to lose it.

"Are you trying to get out of this?" he'll probe like a judge, which isn't a very romantic way to talk to your sweetheart.

He doesn't admit what the Rio Grande's like, but it's got fate threaded through its water, and every now and then, that river changes lives. Martha got pregnant just by going there. Well, and she got in. But still, wading in the river and swimming has never gotten a woman pregnant before, and no one could understand it, especially not her husband, (impotent) Jim.

Of course, I won't bring that up now. Last night was Rusty and Jim's pool night, like every Thursday since the divorce. After all this time, Jim still doesn't ask about the baby. The last time he talked to Martha was when we were all at Applebee's and he said little Anthony wasn't his, in a loud speech ending with "cuckold!" Later in the bathroom, Martha swore to me the river had made Jim's sperm take hold. She said she felt it happen inside her when a wave wet her to the waist, and a brightness flashed under her skin, beneath her bellybutton, in her depths. A light turning on, and that was it.

Back when I met them five years ago at the fall bar-b-que, Jim was sweet and a little awkward, keeping his arm around Martha's shoulder almost the entire day. He introduced her to me as his "prize," but once the river got her pregnant, he turned cold and hard as a winter lock frozen shut. Martha moved away to Lake Shasta for warmth and to live by her family, but I saw her in my dream just two nights ago. She was laughing in slow-motion and cradling a golden baby with fertile green eyes, shining like 1st prize. I took it as a good sign.

A more spiritual man might thank the potent river that blessed his wife. Jim's an import car mechanic with ten-hour workdays, and when the pieces didn't match up, he made his decision. It's never occurred to him that the river's powers are real, that anything could be governed by rules he didn't know about. He's Rusty's closest friend, other than me: Rusty's fiancé, minus a ring.

I *didn't* lose it on purpose. Makes me think of that lost boy on the fliers outside of Albertson's who went missing years ago; I'm sure he didn't mean to walk by the riverside and disappear. The police said, "probable abduction," but you know what I thought? Maybe the river men wanted him. From the tales my great-grandmother told me when I was a girl, it's quite an honor if the river men take you. They'll make you immortal, or super-powered, or happy—that's actually the part I wish I could remember. My great-grandma was as tall as me when she died when I was seven, and I've forgotten some details. Nobody else talks like her. I've listened.

I didn't know that lost boy, but he did have an interesting walk, really bouncy. I saw his class once on a field trip downtown, and he stood out. His dark head bopped up higher than the others', and his loose hands flopped at his sides like fish. It was an eccentric walk, you could say. Maybe that's what the river men liked about him.

I have lots of eccentricities for a river man to like. It seems they also like gold. *Of course,* I feel guilty about losing my engagement ring. Its absence casts me as the forgetful female I'm always trying to convince Rusty I'm not.

And now he's pulling in the drive. I meant to do the dishes.

The mirror over the stove says I'm a windy red tangle, but that's what buns are for. I fix my hair, lick my lips to make them brighter, and change my hazel eyes from brown hesitation to green welcoming. The lock slides back, Rusty opens the front door, and I remember I need to stop caring about what he thinks.

"Hello, my love," he says, and sets his shoulder-slung briefcase by the wall. "Hi, sweetie," I answer, fold my hands behind me, and lean back against kitchen doorway. I can still see the outdoorsman hidden under his office clothes, his masked strength. He walks down the long hallway, his shiny businessman shoes tapping girlishly on the hard wood floor. With each step, his gelled hair lifts and falls like a wing on his forehead. I briefly wonder where our 20s went and when we got so domestic.

"Finally home," Rusty says and sighs. I turn my face up, lips puckered. He encircles my waist, and for a second there, his nose mashes mine, our mouths seal, and I can't breathe. A panic flutter goes through me, but then he turns his head and my nostrils work again. Knees bent, he pins me to the wall with his foot-taller body, and I'm unimpressed. Till magically, his hand slides down my back and simply cups my ass, just right. He draws back, waits an inch above my neck, and breathes.

And I'm panting. My body becomes a hot red ribbon draped around him, like I'm a red vein leading to his heart. Each day I'm floored by his spell, amazed that it's happening. I'm powerless against the effects; I'd think I'd be more rational, yet it takes so little and I starve for him, him, *him*.

He pulls away just when I want him, and I feel like a sucker. He wipes his mouth and runs his fingers through his hair to crack the gel and muss it natural. "You want a beer, baby?" he asks, walking to the refrigerator. He kicks off his fancy man shoes and nudges them under the counter. Head in the fridge, he asks, "Yes or no?"

"My engagement ring fell in the river," I answer, though I could've sworn I was going to say yes.

He slumps half-inside the fridge for a minute, then emerges with two beers, sets them on the counter, pops off one cap with his lighter, and sets the bottle cap down gently. "It slipped off," I say. He hands over the open beer without turning; I take a sip. He opens his beer, sets down the cap, finally drinks. Staring at the counter, he asks, "Don't you want to marry me?"

"Come on," I say. "I didn't mean to. I went to take a walk by the river this morning. It looks like all the geese are back. I was halfway back across the little fishing bridge when the ring slipped off and fell in. It was weird, Rusty, because it's humid today and my fingers are even swollen. That ring had a snug fit, but right then it just… slipped off."

I leave out how mesmerizing its circle was when it dawdled as it sank, drifting lightly back and forth, as above, my small dry hand reached toward its escape.

He sighs, then drinks his whole beer in one go. It's a noisy business with a lot of swallowing sounds. When the river swallowed my ring, it made the quietest "blip."

Rusty gives a breathy burp and asks in a resigned tone, "Shouldn't we go look for it?"

I shut my eyes, lift my beer, and take three long swallows. As I drink, I imagine the Rio Grande with all those phantom river men swimming through the waves like silky ropes, and one river man carries on his back the lost boy with the bouncy walk, sitting straight up. When they rise over a wave, the boy sees me; he raises both of his floppy hands in hello. He doesn't fall off the river man, even without holding on, and his left hand glitters in the sunlight with my gold ring.

"I doubt we'll find it," I say, and give a burp of my own. "But if you want, we can try."

Rusty shakes his head and I watch the muscles in his cheeks shift as he bites down hard. "I want to know you'll be mine," he says with the same thick-voiced earnest drawl he had at fifteen. We met when I was on my family's Rio Grande fishing trip; I crossed the little bridge as he was reeling in his third catfish. He had the ability to pull fish after fish from the water and caught two more as we talked, plus he was cute, so when he offered to cook me up that very catfish of hello, I ate it. Now I wonder, maybe eating his fish is what did it. Because I changed; love got in me and made me stupider. My intuition doesn't work as well around him, or I suppose I don't follow it as much. In certain ways, it leaves me wide open.

I've left him before; this last time I was gone four years. I had another life, with my own waffle garden. I was independent and square-shouldered; I felt wise. I'd moved on, but not really. Each time, the curling memory of him hooks me, I think of him more and more, and long for that mysterious way we're attached. It always catches me eventually, and then I seek him out, leave my coming harvest, and return like I did last year, while he remains close to the Rio Grande, like he's still standing on that little bridge, reeling me in. I've never loved anyone like I have Rusty. With such a solid claim on me, it's like I never had a choice.

"Just be mine," requests my river man now, in the same whispered urgency he said it with then, and I want to run away. Then, he touches my waist, and a current runs through the magnet of me.

Observe how I turn to *yes*, and those are *my* hands that climb his back, as he licks my neck, kissing my hair wet.

Wrapped in his embrace, I watch the water tumble down the carpeted stairs, swash over the kitchen floor, and eddy around our ankles. Soon, our house is hazy green and roaring. It's flooding with the river's uncontrollable currents, come to return his ring to him.

*

Under the Bridge

"Can you stop drowning now?" I never said that to her. I thought it, though.

"Nope. I don't believe so." Erica didn't say that outright, but with people you know really well, whole conversations can happen in silence, and moments can be poems.

We were three years into our relationship, when my resilient, beautiful partner suffered a death in the family and swiftly fell apart. The way I see it, we have bridges in our lives that span the distance between before and after, and in between are the chasms of tragedy. Everyone worries they won't get across. Well, Erica fell from that bridge, alright, and then she just stayed underwater.

I remember the phone ringing at midnight. As soon as she heard the news, she was soaking. I watched little puddles form by her collarbones. First, the sheets drenched with tears, and then, she sank and drifted down into her personal abyss.

"Erica," I said, "don't go." She wouldn't respond or even meet my eye, so I held my breath, dove under the sheet and into her deep-sea sadness, and kissed each tattooed petal of her sternum's red rose.

Drowned beneath the water, her skin was like marble, luminescent, and even her colorful tattoos dulled. Her blond hair swept across her face, stirring with currents. I kissed her through the corn-silk, chanting consolations, but with her ears waterlogged, she seemed to only hear her own heartbeat. "Hey," I said anyway, "I love you."

When I was a girl, my best friend and I would play with death and past lives, trying to go back and remember, getting ourselves freaked out and worked up. One story was I'd been a beagle dog and my friend was a deer in the road, eyes glazed over, charmed by an approaching car's headlights. I ran from the woods to scare her off and save her, and then of course, the car hit me instead and I died. And oh, how we cried, mourning the beautiful sacrifice. We were nine, and somehow all our stories gave me the tragic ending. Erica reminded me of my little kid best friend sobbing on my canopy bed, not wanting to leave the beautiful sorrow behind.

On Dia de los Muertos, we walked through the gold

cottonwoods and laid together in the sand next to the Rio Grande, listening to the licking water sounds and bird pips. Azure sky above, water lapping at the shore, I held Erica for hours, till things got confusing. For a while, I imagined us as two skeletons who'd each been lost in the river for countless years, and the waves were swaying and bringing us closer, grazing us past, till at last we met, our ribs interlocked, and *click* went our hips. I kissed Erica's neck and whispered her name and imagined my body full of stars.

Afterwards, that gorgeous vision haunted me, so I told her about it, how beautifully the waves ended our loneliness, how we'd fit together while the water carried us. She said nothing, of course (the girl had her patterns), just held me tighter. I guessed it had been a weird thing to say.

That's when I started considering bridge-crossing methods. How *does* someone get over something like this? "You're right," I told her, giving a head-nod toward her tears. "That accident was awful, and it tore you apart. But life goes on… Follow an interest," I said. "Don't you have a hobby?" She didn't reply, but soon after, she started a community college photography course.

Photography grew into her whole world, but I didn't mind losing her to it, because she couldn't get the right shot if she dripped on the camera, which finally convinced her to curb her incessant drowning. At the semester's end, her voice creaked, breaking our living room's quiet. "My class is giving a final show," Erica said. She arched back her neck and stared at the ceiling, then exhaled. "Be my date?"

On the photography room's concrete walls, her classmates' artworks were displayed like rectangular windows into a hundred worlds. Erica's windows were divided into two territories. One side was monochrome contact sheets repeated like a mantra, small photos of a 1960s couple. The woman I recognized as her mother from photo albums, though I never got to meet her. The young couple was in love, on a road trip, happy—unlike us.

These were offset by photos documenting our recent forays to Blue Lake, the woods of turning aspens, the bank of the Rio Grande. Then, I saw that she'd weirdly altered every print. Each shot she'd taken of us now contained only her, under her mourning veil of hair.

Each portrait of me, sprawled on the clover hill, winking at dusk amongst the sage, had lost its me and become a landscape. The shock was like careening through a guardrail, arcing down to the river below.

"Why would you erase me?" I asked under the florescent lighting.

"I miss you," Erica whispered, looking just left of my face. She closed her ice-blue eyes. The tattooed star on her neck pulsed. "I keep waiting for you."

I checked to see how late I was, as if I wore a watch, but when I pushed up my sleeve, my skin pushed up too and revealed my clean forearm bones. My wrist bones were arranged like an intricate white cairn, and beside them was a pile of pomegranate seeds, like a red reflection. My movement disturbed the pile, and one seed rolled along my arm bone with the gesture.

I watched the ruby seed rolling diagonally, and after all these months, I knew.

So, next to Erica's picture-windows, I tilted up her patient chin and kissed my sweet lost love. "Baby," I said, "thanks for waiting up. I'm home." And it was like a magnetic difference. It was so good and gorgeous; I began to rise. Up from my coat, my bones lifted through the room as a calavera, through the ceiling, into the sky. There, I kited above the building as spires of moonlight shone through my ribs.

Meanwhile, down in the photography room, Erica buoyed up from her depths. She pushed her pale hair from her face, as if she were breaking through water, and coughed to clear her lungs. Blinking, she licked her lips, like she'd just woken up at the art show.

"Man," she said, "am I thirsty."

The refreshment table was in the far corner of the room, stacked with ice-filled buckets holding beading bottles of water, iced tea, and beer. Wine bottles crowded the table. A tall glass bowl of icy horchata shared sweat beads with a copper cauldron of watermelon juice. All were laid out like sparkling elixirs. A revolution occurred in Erica's slight expressions.

Some steps we take travel parallel terrain. I saw it all happen, down below me. That beautiful woman strode across the room to get herself the refreshment she needed. And with each footstep, Erica advanced across her own fateful bridge, till she reached its other side. Once there, she pulled a transparent cup from the tall stack on the table waiting for her and filled it with ice from a silver scoop. Then, she went for the watermelon juice.

Her stance shifted into grace and her eyes cleared. A birdcall shrieked and echoed down the school hallway, the staccato racket of a roadrunner. There it was again. Erica volleyed her cup in the trash, got out her camera, and took off to explore. The harsh birdcall clattered again from further down the hall, and Erica started jogging. As her foot left the classroom doorway, my silvery kite tether to the building broke, and I lifted with the quick dark magnetism pulling me higher, past the blurring stars, into what comes next.

*

We've Already Been Invented

"Let me tell you about your hair," the businessman announced from the next table over at Burger King, a piece of French fry on his lip.

The guy was so bald; that's what got Kyle, who was about to take a sip of Mountain Dew and froze, with the straw inches from his mouth, like he'd been caught in the basilisk's gaze. If he were still in the Dungeons & Dragons: Baldur's Gate, 1999 edition computer game he'd been playing almost continuously since it came out earlier that year, he'd have to wait powerless for two plays till he could move again.

The guy didn't hold the suspense. "We *invented* your hair." He was real impressed with his joke, alright. His three friends in suits laughed, their gray-shadowed cheeks full of combo meals. They were attorneys, or maybe corporate salesmen, men with their eyes on the prize. Baldy raised his eyebrows at his seatmates in triumph, licked the fry from his lip, and confirmed to Kyle, sitting at the neighboring table, "We did." As if Baldy even knew Kyle. As if Baldy even had hair.

Kyle locked eyes with him, slid the straw between his lips, and loudly slurped Mountain Dew as if it were Stone-to-Flesh elixir. He gave a deep burp.

The man in a suit picked up three French fries, swiped them through his streaky ketchup pile, and said, "We invented your burp too." He popped the fries in his mouth, chewed, then added, "And your insolence." He nodded as he swallowed, and his portly tribe chuckled and continued inhaling the burgers that maintained their buoyant midriffs.

Kyle flipped back his long bangs, then messed his hair into a shaggy spectacle, points going everywhere. His friend Brian watched it all in his heavy-lidded stoner way. Who's to say how much Brian took in; he might have still been back in the D&D game paused in the basement.

Kyle turned to the man, crazy-haired, and lisped, "Sorry, perv. I don't dig the old guys." He squeaked out an elongated kiss, winked, and took a humungous bite of Whopper.

Baldy raised his own Whopper in toast and also ate a bite.

The men at his table started another conversation, but Kyle could still feel Baldy's attention. He wondered if the guy could smell weed on them, if he even knew the smell of it. Kyle and Brian hot-boxed the game room right before leaving the house, so chances were they reeked.

"If I had my choice," Kyle thought, "which spell would I blast him with now?" Fireball was the winner, and he imagined the fake-wood-paneled restaurant blazing white, right before the *boom* and flashing orange, *boom boom boom, boomboom.* He was advanced level now and his Fireball spells got six explosions instead of the novice three or four. "Yeah, I'd annihilate you," he thought at the guy, his mind full of insidious flames as he chewed.

Baldy swallowed loudly, adjusted his pant leg, and asked over to their table, "Let me guess: you go drinking in the woods?" He scratched his scalp with his middle finger. "You guys make bonfires and smoke big joints and screw girls in the dark under the cottonwoods?"

"Why are you talking to me, man?!" Kyle yelled, eyebrows diagonal. He shoved the last of his burger in his mouth, stood up, and swiped his burger wrapper, full of fries and ketchup, to the floor. He grabbed his skateboard, and Brian, sensing the trend, balled up his burger paper with half his meal inside and stuffed it in his sweatshirt pocket. There was a short fry left on the table, and with a shrug, Brian came to life. Spotting the opportunity, he took aim and flicked the fry at the businessmen's table.

It hit the table edge and fell. "Have fun, tough guys," Baldy said and ate three more fries.

Kyle and Brian's hands slapped open the Burger King doors, and they skated down the mall hallway, wheels clacking on the ridges of the tiles. Brian pulled some fries from his pocket and ate as he skated. And it was stupid, but as they passed the regularly spaced yellow wall lamps, Kyle couldn't stop thinking about that damn guy's woods, with the trees flickering in orange light, not from Fireballs but bonfires, the woods where that guy went when he was young, when his friends passed him a joint, and then he drifted away from the fire like smoke, to lay beneath the tall trees and stars with a girl, probably someone classy like Susana, who bummed a cigarette at lunch.

Kyle and Brian skated the three flat streets to his house and thundered down to the basement game room, still muggy with stale pot smoke. Kyle pulled his kicked-out chair back to the computer, and Brian moved the mouse to wake the screen. His thumb hit the space bar, and their D&D game restarted as if they'd never left it.

"Damn Baldy doesn't even have hair," Kyle fumed as he shot an ogre herd. "You don't know me," imagining his targets were that guy and his bloodsucking friends screaming like howling lampreys. What really sucked was that it had sounded fun, but this side of the city didn't even have woods anymore—they'd been flattened by subdivisions and strip-malls. He'd never sat by a bonfire, looking up at the cottonwoods with a girl in his arms, and that guy had.

And one day, Kyle would go bald.

*

Our Master of Psalmody

The neuter down the street, Lee, is a master of psalmody. He used to sing her psalms in church, with liquid, heartbreaking grace, and women swayed flat-heeled shoes; men nodded thick necks. Everyone shone. And yet, unsure of which role to consider the slender brunette in tan linen pants, no one sat too close or offered conversation. My parents and neighbors couldn't decide if they should be flirtatious or macho, discuss the latest mini-series or who would win the playoffs. They grew nervous to mention car repairs or romance, began to second-guess their own roles, and quickly looked away. But they did love to hear Lee sing.

Our preacher was a sweaty, potato-bodied man whose face inflamed red and shiny when he spoke, but for all his enthusiasm, he was tortuously boring. So this, coupled with Lee's glissando, made his awaited honey psalms our rich dessert after each dutiful service. The preacher, possessed of plain sight, of course noticed their rankings, and his brow wrinkled in a tight pinch.

Nowadays, you can only hear Lee's voice sweetening the air if you walk past her open window. You see, all those years, no one discussed his songs' lyrics. The elongated words sounded religious, till the jealous preacher tape-recorded them. Then he went home, hitched up his pant legs, and sat on his carpet to listen. The next Sunday, Lee wasn't there, and hasn't been there since. Turns out, her holy psalms sang of silk stockings and saffron underwear, sweat beads on upper lips, cat cry moans, bellies on backs, breath on skin.

She/he/Lee has no traditional gender, no sexual drive or equipment, yet sings angelically the details of lust. I grew up with those songs about undone buttons and upper thighs. For six years, my body heightened and ripened, and reposed once a week, among usually hard women, like Mrs. Green and Ms. Gunter, gone flushed and quick-breathed; the row of old mechanic men turned beacon-eyed; the leaned back school kids, mouths parted; and all my other transported neighbors.

After thinking many attentive hours about it, I believe Lee's psalms are a kind of primal scream, a healing erotic eruption. She balances celibacy by transcribing passion and tonguing it out. Then, (the rush!) he releases her songs to touch us en masse, in mass, while we're most controlled and polite.

I wouldn't say the discovery offended the churchgoers. I bet most knew what words were sung like wet passion prayers within the church walls, and were privately excited by the act's illegality and their quiet complicity. To this day, there's a short, sacred radius around Lee like a chapel of libido, and people gather, regular as a weekly service, but more willingly attended.

Men and women appear on his lawn like mushrooms, to search the grass for imaginary lost items, or casually retie their already tight laces. Grandmothers, gangly boys, middle-aged men, and young wives come close to listen, blush and smile. But they don't talk to Lee, who sings for them anyway. They just wouldn't know what to say.

*

Youth

She will never find me. Alice keeps looking, but I keep changing. Today she thinks I'm a picture in a brass oval frame she threw out by accident, maybe two weeks ago when she tipped the desk and slid everything off into the bin. She was upset that day; sometimes these things happen.

She digs through the trashcans lining the road. The Tuesday morning sun has just blazed its way over the mountains, and the car windshields are bright as dentists' lights. The garbage men should be here any minute, but Alice doesn't rush. Her pointed straw hat noses around like a tan bird beak, as her gnarled hands peck and sort through her neighbor's trash, looking for that oval frame.

Each Tuesday morning, it's something else. According to her, I'm all sorts of things. Three weeks ago, I was the poppy red umbrella she twirled in the rain when she walked to her old job downtown. Last week, I was an antique clothespin doll she made her mother when she was five. She searched for me for hours, beginning in the dark morning with her dedicated crooked fingers, pushing aside clonking cans and pizza crusts, worried that my felt dress and neckerchief would get stained by someone's marinara.

This week, I'm a picture in a brass frame edged in curlicues, with a crack in the glass going across her sister's mouth and into her own temple—an unfortunate break, but no reason to throw away something good.

"Jeanine," her voice creaks into the trashcan. "Where are you?" Her bird beak bobs as she calls for her sister, like they're still as young as they were in the hand-colored black-and-white—"Jeanine, come out"—as if she can push aside a cereal box and her little sister will spring free like a Jack-in-the-Box, with her ringlets bouncing.

She pulls up an old mop with matted strings, and then pokes it into the tightly packed trash can, again and again like she's aerating the garbage, or trying to get it to awaken. Then, bent down with her hat's peak aimed at the street, lips inches from an oil change receipt, she whispers, "I said I was sorry. Your Rodney only thought I was pretty, which is not a crime. I wouldn't ever'of stole him."

She waits for an answer—a whole minute she waits, first with eyes shut, and then open, reading, "$39.99 Standard, Plus Emissions."

Officiously, she straightens and inserts the mop back in the can. She withdraws it with both hands and jabs the matted mop head in a different spot.

This completed, she pulls the mop out and hoists it over her shoulder like a musket as she heads across the street toward the other side's bank of cans. She may have better luck there.

A kraken screech cuts the air from the next block over, followed by a groan of metal parts scraping, a hydraulic wheeze, and the clatter of a garbage bin landing on the street. Alice stops on the yellow center line and faces the racket. "Jeanine," she says, "you have to come out. They're coming." She huffs through her nose in annoyance at the things she puts up with and proceeds to the next trashcan's investigation, her bird beak darting.

The kraken screeches louder, and scrapes and wheezes and clatters, and then the garbage truck rounds the corner, brakes, jerks forward, staggering closer. Now just four houses away. Alice moves on to the next bin, leaving the mop towering from the previous one, matted head watching.

She can't figure out where to find me. She only knows that garbage truck wants to take me away again, stealing her life and her memories Tuesday by Tuesday, year after year, until she has nothing to hold onto to help her remember.

A couple feet away, the truck halts with an excited pert scream and hisses in warning. A man in a blue uniform rides on the back of it. Alice's bird beak lifts, aimed up at the sky (God and everyone will hear her fury); the man drops to the street.

"Get away from me. I don't believe in you anymore," she screams back. A swoop of wet gray hair is in her mouth, and her eyes are wide, dead serious. "You can't keep stealing from me."

The weary strong-armed man swings the contents of one, two, three containers into the back of the truck, and softer, she says, "I don't believe in you." He pulls himself up on the outer railing and the truck passes Alice, gives an earsplitting screech, brakes, and he descends again to toss in more contents. So, the truck continues on, stealing all that's been used, leaving her in the street by the hollow Tuesday morning trashcans.

*

Sulphur Steam

Up on the mountain, we hang out in abandoned buildings, places where stories fill the holes in the walls. The old teepee was on the bottom of that ridge, before lightning struck. Now all that's left is the charred platform. Harry's cabin is up the road, but he sometimes returns, with his shotgun, dogs, and paranoia, so I stay away. The trailer sits low in the valley. With electricity, it's the homiest of the buildings, half-wild, its library varied as the friends who've passed through: books on metaphysics, botany, geology, and astronomy; plus a bounty of porn and pine mice. The door's unlocked, and some windows don't close, but the vital mountain's so gorgeous, it feels only natural to let it inside.

Above, atop the steep hill, is the old silver bullet trailer left alone and gone feral, which Mikky and his cousins, and Rain and I took over and named The Witch's Brew. Afternoons when the giant snowflakes whiten the forest, that's where we hide out. We run an extension cord up from the trailer, and make coffee, music, and art from random junk. We're real-life magicians.

Down the road, that's the log cabin, with scalloped, golden pine walls, an iron wood-burning stove, and an unfinished roof that opens the attic to the stars and sky. Animals lived among the altar stones and carved chalices. Rain and I clear them out and clean up, carry in water jugs, and sleep on the regal bed in our zipped-together sleeping bags.

On Halloween night, when the veil between worlds is thinnest, we drink hard lemonade and whisky with Blacky, a new friend. The candles burn, pinon sap smolders sweetly on the cast iron stovetop, and our intimacies bind. We're candid, affectionate, drunk. Blacky confesses to horrendous teenage violence, says he's been a bad person for centuries. Then we're all remembering a ship from another life, in the 1800's. Blacky was a pirate, and we were sailing passengers. He hugs Rain tight, confesses, "I'm so sorry for killing you."

His tattooed arms gesture my delicate Victorian gown; he says I'd looked so beautiful, he'd wished he were a different man. Blacky holds me, remembering across lifetimes. He says he's ashamed for what he did to me, stares at my lips, my eyes. He'd hated himself for it. We all embrace, forgive, in the flame-lit cabin like a ship lost at sea.

At midnight, Rain, Blacky, and I walk to a steamy meadow with protruding wooden posts. They're next to the sulphur hot springs and fumarole, the last remnants of a 1920's bathhouse and inn that burned to the ground decades ago. The moon shines white, cold, and huge. Then Blacky picks up a stake and starts bashing the old foundation posts. And it's unlike me, but I pound the old wood too, breaking and splintering the pieces that remain, as destructive as time passing.

*

You Could Measure It Perfectly

When I open my front door, a beam of streetlight shines from behind me into the dark living room, and someone's standing right there. My blood chills, but it's just my silhouette in an orange rectangle of streetlight on the far wall. I walk in, matching steps with my shadow in the orange box. Then I kick the door shut, and everything disappears.

Even in the dark, I know where to step. I pride myself on this and lean around, reach out, feel for the lamp's cord and flick the light on, then step back around the table's pointy edge.

But of course, the table's gone. In the light, I remember it's been gone for weeks. If you were to watch my movements, you could tell how high the table was and how wide, you could measure it perfectly through the way I avoid this one spot.

My lover Rich didn't give it a second thought. He's athletic and careless, like a handsome young tomcat. He was arched back, scratching around the new flame tattoo he'd just gotten on his belly, when he told me the table wasn't a big loss, and besides it got in the way of the TV.

It was an old table, a $4 yard sale score that, for the past three months, I piled high with books. First, I added mythology books, then etymologies, a big book of baby names, and then a recent gift from my mother, on the benefits of breastfeeding. The table had low corners I used to bang my shins on till I learned when to lean. Till it became a part of my room, even in the dark, even when it's gone.

I tip backwards and thump onto my crinkling plastic orange couch; my feet give a second landing, and I stare forward. Without the table, I have a clear pathway to the TV. Someone spying through the window would think I'm watching a show. As if I'm fine, as if there's something on.

Nothing's on; it's just this unblinking TV eye.

I punch the vinyl couch cushion.

"Elly. Is that you?" Rich calls from the bedroom. A stupid question. Anyone could say yes and lie. I want to answer in a deep man's voice, "Yes, that's right, Elly here."

Instead I say nothing.

"Nothing."

What?" he calls, and gives a critical huff from his nose. It's enough to get him moving. Ceiling lights come on, charting his path as he walks heavily down the hallway, unaware: of what's there, or not there, or still there but only in my mind.

In just his tube socks, curly-haired Rich leans, hip cocked against the wall, wearing a spectator's expression. I focus on being as uninteresting as possible, a person on an orange couch. I try using my mental abilities to make the orange a more boring color. Look away, Rich, go away.

He stares on.

"That little kid came by for you," he says, lifts his chin, and loudly scratches the stubble on his neck. "The toy-car kid that lives downstairs. The Russian one." He massages his shoulder, and I know that aloof, confident expression too well. It's how he always looks when he leaves me alone here in the storyline. "I don't know what he wanted," he says, pressing his fingers along his muscles and giving a private, contented smile.

Rich's face doesn't flinch when he says "little kid," "lives," "wanted." Loaded words these days.

I rub slow circles over my belly, with my face opaque, blue eyes unblinking, while I telepathically state, 'You would've made the worst dad in the world.' Out loud I say, "Alix probably wanted a round of Flying Cars in the Courtyard... Or maybe he wanted an end table. Too bad if he does because the end table's already gone."

Rich shakes his head like I'm his dumb kid brother. He bends, inspecting a bite on his leg, and asks, "What the hell would the Russian kid want with an end table?"

It's like I get an itch too, to wake him up. Next thing I know, I grab the couch cushions next to me and stand, waving them like heavy orange flags. And the words are out: "Or have you even *noticed*?" My voice reverberates in the hollow room. "That it's been gone, and I keep forgetting that somehow, and getting reminded again, and it's just going to keep being gone!"

I hurl both cushions at him. They bounce off his legs, and he stumbles over them, face red and eyebrows scrunched. "Look, it's been three weeks," Rich says, and grips my arm tight enough to bruise. "When are you going to be normal? I know you have hormones and all. But you're really losing it," he lectures, as I die and fall on the floor.

     A layer of me does anyway, the part full of all that is gone.

     What I wonder is, when I'm crossing the room late at night, how long am I going to keep stepping over that body there?

*

Why the Moon

"Is there enough time?" I asked. For truth, I meant. There isn't always.

Rogelio was leaving for work, running late. He'd been gathering his papers, about to go when I asked him, "How do you really feel?" And he stopped: his moment for me.

Rogelio was a man veiled by modesty and mild adjectives. I found him most honest when naked, so it made sense when he said, "I'll show you," and took off his jacket. He lifted his shirt, then grabbed my hand and pressed it to his warm chest.

"Hold here," he said. I held on, palming one side of his sleek ribcage. He held the other fan of ribs and pulled. Crack, his body opened up.

There in the center of his chest was a little boy riding a stallion made of fire. Flame-licking mane and hooves glowing blue. The horse stamped back and forth, eager to run. The boy shone bright white in the glare.

Air rushed in through the crack in his chest. It maddened the horse's flames; I heard the roar of burning. The stallion glared around with wild blue eyes and shook his head. The little boy tightened his hold on the burning mane.

Rogelio jerked away from me, hunched down and shoved his chest closed with both hands. Crack. He pulled down his shirt, smoothed it over his belly with its soft line of hair and then stood beside me, mortal and panting, looking at the ground, recovering his breath.

The world was all earth tones compared to that burning. I missed seeing the colors of heat and light.

He exhaled one last time, put back on his jacket, and regained composure. Looked at me with calm brown eyes, a Geology teacher's eyes. "I have to go to work now." Smiled mild and kindly.

I gripped his arm, expecting the touch to burn. It didn't. His pliant bicep, not too muscular. "Show me again," I whispered.

Rogelio's eyebrows lowered. "No," he said disappointedly, shaking his shaggy black hair. "No, I have to go. My committee's waiting; I can't be late." He slung his bag over his shoulder.

But his chest's bright grotto vision outshone everything else in all the gravity and order around me. "Please," I urged like a flametip, and I wanted to set fire to the entire damp world.

"I can't." He craned his neck as he fixed the twisted strap of his bag. "I don't want to do it again," he said to his shoulder, then flicked his gaze up to me. "I'll see you when I get home," and he kissed my cheek.

I watched him and wondered, Who is this mild earthy creature speaking pebbles and moss, algae water? Opening the door, turning the doorknob's lock between his fingers.

"Wait!" I called from the foyer. He turned and smiled like a mother's I love you, and slowly shut the locked door behind him.

But *I* was speaking to that boy riding the burning horse. I was calling to the moment when he cracked himself open. That passionate wildfire was true, somewhere inside him. I could tell I wouldn't see it, not like that, ever again.

It was enough, that one moment. I stayed with him for years and years, waiting, like the moon circling the earth. At night I escaped to the backyard, to stare at the sky and smolder luminously with my pent-up life force. There in the silent darkness, I learned the secret of the moon, why it pulls the tides. It's the molten fire inside the earth it craves, and the moon goes around and around, vigilantly trying to draw that fire back out.

*

Wind in a Ring Box

The maroon velvet ring box trembled, making a rat-a-tat-tat on the table. I watched it with a raised eyebrow. "What is it?" I asked. "That's for you," Ravi said, like an informative engineer. He leaned back in his dining chair and braided his fingers over his belly. My skin flashed with heat, then cold; I bit my bottom lip. "Why's it shaking?" I asked. "Maybe it's scared," he teased, and pushed it across the dining table with his fingertip. Then it did its subtle dance on the table ledge before me, like a wee tap-dancer on a stage. When I thought about it that way, it wasn't as intimidating, so I laid my linen napkin next to my plate and picked up the box. It quivered against my palm like a finch with a quick heartbeat.

I cracked open the lid, and WOOSH! The entire West Wind erupted. I flew backward, standing upright with my brown dress snapping, and the wee box fell to the ground, still roaring its invisible force. I swept to the far side of the room, where the door was left open, and it seemed I'd be pushed outside to the lawn, and maybe on down the street. So I started pedaling, mid-air, doing a sort of dogpaddle. Meanwhile, my love had gotten down on one knee, offering the ring box on his palm. My hair roared up high and side-to-side, as I worked my arms and legs, managing to stay indoors, and then I kicked high like Mother-May-I steps, and breast stroked my arms, making incremental progress in his direction. Ravi knelt on the tile with a romantic expression and didn't seem to notice my struggle.

He said, "Will you do me the honor of marrying me?" I had to watch his lips to hear him, because the wind screamed piercingly unless I turned my head just right. I tried to smile with my mouth closed, so the wind wouldn't blow my lips all over the place. Squinting, I made my way to the center of the room, trying to see inside the box. He puckered his eyebrows, concerned that I hadn't answered, so I grabbed a nearby table edge and shoved off hard. I struggled to stretch out my left arm. "Ye-e-e-sss," I vibrated, like I was talking in front of a fan. He pulled the ring from the box, a silver flash, and then slid it on my ring finger.

The room went still, and I fell on the floor. He bent over me in surprise, and I flushed excitedly, opened my mouth, and sang an inhuman, rippling birdsong. Good God, I wondered, pushing myself back upright, what have I gotten into now? He smiled at me like a husband, and I touched that forceful silver and diamond ring upon my finger, wondering where all that wind went. Later, I would think it entered my years, because after that, they just flew by.

*

Wish on the Ring's Eye

A RING, swaying on a strand of hair, high in a tree, hits against the trunk and makes a—*ting*—marking the beginning. The blond knot unwinds, and the silver ring slips free. It's falling…

Yesterday, it arrived at the tree's top when Isobel carried the ring up, sat on the highest thick branch, dandling the ring on a strand of her hair, swaying it back and forth like her own hypnotism. Just before dusk, the girl put her lips around the ring's center, and gave a kiss, making a wish that cast through her like light through a keyhole. She let the beautiful urge through and imagined the days passing as potently as life felt up in the tree. She saw herself as a sun queen.

Potential shone in the air like gold dust motes, taking notice, watching her powerful belief. She tied a knot in the hair and hung it from a twig, and left the wish swaying below. Then, she trotted home.

In time, the moon rose like a levitating coin from behind the magician's dark velvet horizon, floating past the tree's branches, past new buds spiraled closed and soft caterpillars creeping. Then the moon saw the delicately hung ring and felt the true wish spinning round its perimeter. Leaving a tracer, the moon pulled itself over and shimmied higher so that the silver ring framed its lunar brightness.

The circlet wish raced faster around the ring, an agent of change building speed from that change-master, faster—till the moon eased on away to look at other things. Then the wound-up wish slowed and dragged round the ring's edge, humming like a Tibetan singing bowl. Asleep in bed, Isobel rolled over and moaned the same tone. The moon winked in appreciation and kept moving past her window.

It was the wind that lifted the ring from its twiggy perch, come morning—the jealous wind whose fingers are too thin to wear a ring and is only given love trinkets instead, flower petals and small paper notes, but never such a commitment as the tree's silver. The wind simply huffed, and the ring lifted.

It glinted, dropping through the morning light, and the moon squinted between the mountain peaks to spy its flash of silver. The spiral buds on branches all started to unfurl, and the little girl woke mid-dream, and spoke:

"Magic of life, marry me," Isobel incants now, forcefully. A powerful, yet vague enough enchantment that all nearby inherent magic gathers tight as a cattail's pressed pollen. She stands on her bed and blows, and it spreads every which way.

Up high, Isobel wears a radiant halo; the sun waits behind her head, like a beau by her window. Over in the woods, *ting*, hits the silver ring against a rock in the ground. It bounces in a high arc, flipping, falls, and marries the grass that pushes through the ring like a finger.

* * *

With Thanks

Many thanks to my mom, who raised me with her charming, unfurling stories, my first storyteller. Deep thanks to Mattie Greenman, my soul bro, for sharing decades of magic and belief with me. His friendship was a candle in my heart that still warms me. Thanks to my dad, who loved thoughtful conversations and my writing passion, and to my brother Sean for his kind encouragement. Thanks to the Plume: A Writer's Companion community, especially Melanie Unruh, Sam Tetangco Ocena, and Jenn Simpson for their woman power and support. Thanks to all my wonderful teachers over the years, including Dan Mueller, Summer Wood, Carol Taylor (third grade), and Donna Peacock (high school English), and to the University of New Mexico MFA program, where I workshopped several of these stories. Much appreciation to Leah Maines and Finishing Line Press for publishing this collection, and to Christen Kincaid for her editorial work. Many thanks to Alexandra Eldridge for sharing her beautiful artwork on the cover. (Find more of her dreamlike work at alexandraeldridge.com.) Thanks to all the writers and creators still sharing their weird, soulful art with this world—you are the antidote. And thank you, Spirit, for your love and presence.

*

(deep curtsy)

Dawn Sperber's stories and poems often focus on magic—the real-life variety—no fancy wands or perfect edges, necessarily. She's a writer, editor, and artist in New Mexico, who's drawn to authenticity and healing and pursuing the mojo that motors us through the challenges. *Now, That's a Trick* is her debut fiction chapbook, based in New Mexico, a collection of flash stories that are "magic and floating, yet rooted in our shared existence." Later this year, Dawn's debut book of poems and drawings, *My Bones Are Love Gifts*, is coming out from Shanti Arts. Her writings have appeared in *Daily Science Fiction, PANK, Hunger Mountain, Bourbon Penn, K'in Literary Journal, We'Moon, Going Down Swinging, Zizzle Lit, NANO Fiction, The Doctor T.J. Eckleburg Review, Annalemma, flashquake, Rosebud, The Pedestal, ONE ART,* and elsewhere. Years ago, she helped with writing conferences hosted by the Taos Summer Writers' Conference and the A Room of Her Own Foundation, and she studied in the University of New Mexico's MFA program, where she held an assistantship as a graduate writing tutor. Now, she's a freelance editor, she reads for *Boulevard Magazine,* and she's a Co-director at Plume: A Writer's Companion, a writing community and literary podcast for women and non-binary writers. Find links to her published stories at dawnsperber.com. On Instagram, she's @pen.paper.light; and on Twitter, she's @DawnSperberEdit. She used to be half-ethers, but now she's up to 80% solid. (Well, depends on the day.)

www.ingramcontent.com/pod-product-compliance
Lightning Source LLC
Chambersburg PA
CBHW052014240626
47153CB00008B/2877